IRWIN THE SOCK

Story by David J. Klein
Illustrations by Shirley V. Beckes

RSVP
RAINTREE
STECK-VAUGHN
P U B L I S H E R S
The Steck-Vaughn Company

Austin, Texas

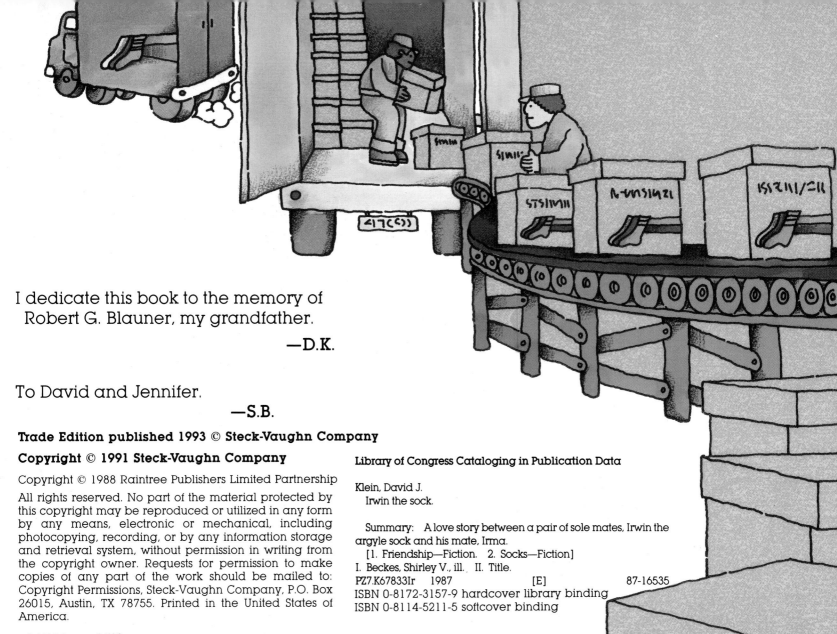

I dedicate this book to the memory of
Robert G. Blauner, my grandfather.

—D.K.

To David and Jennifer.

—S.B.

Trade Edition published 1993 © Steck-Vaughn Company

Copyright © 1991 Steck-Vaughn Company

Copyright © 1988 Raintree Publishers Limited Partnership

5 6 7 8 9   94 93

Library of Congress Number: 87-16535

Library of Congress Cataloging in Publication Data

Klein, David J.
  Irwin the sock.

  Summary: A love story between a pair of sole mates, Irwin the
argyle sock and his mate, Irma.
  [1. Friendship—Fiction.   2. Socks—Fiction]
I. Beckes, Shirley V., ill.   II. Title.
PZ7.K67833Ir   1987   [E]   87-16535
ISBN 0-8172-3157-9 hardcover library binding
ISBN 0-8114-5211-5 softcover binding

My name is Irwin. I am an argyle sock. I am alone and retired now, but I have had a long and exciting life.

I remember when Irma, my mate, and I were created in a textile factory in New England. We were made for each other, our lines and colors perfectly matched.

Our fate was forever sealed in a cellophane wrapper when one day, doubled over and bound, we were squeezed into a packing box and shipped to New York City. The next light we saw was from the display case in the men's department of a ritzy department store. Lying on the shelf, heel to heel and toe to toe, Irma and I were so very happy and, we thought, inseparable.

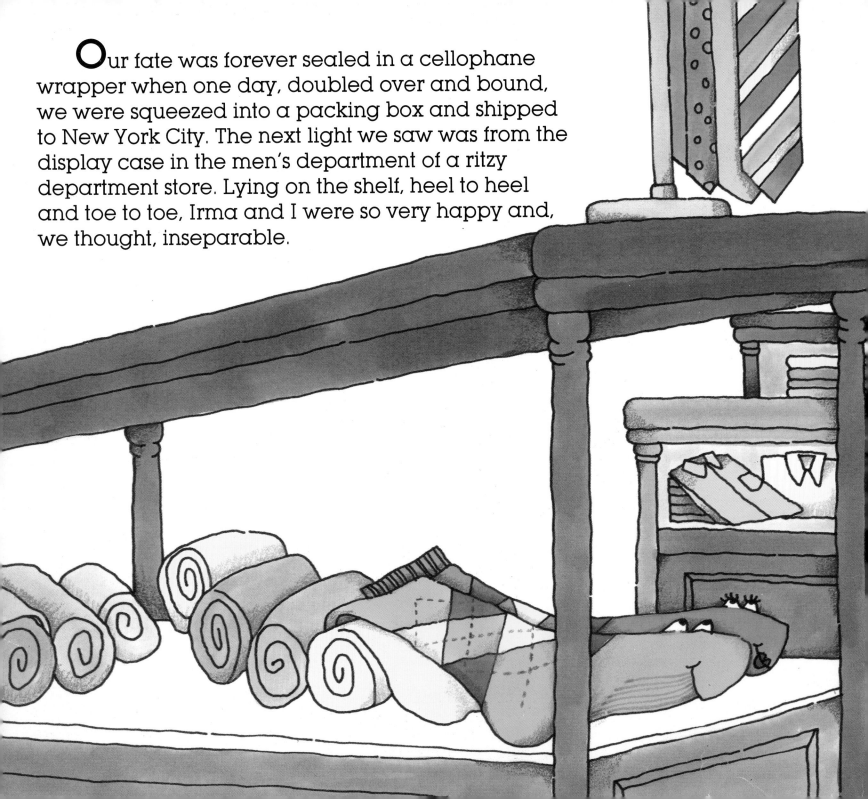

As the weather turned cold, the store became busier. Pretty music played all around. A big man in a funny red suit and hat rang a bell every day for weeks. Shoppers began to grab and snatch our neighbors away, but we stayed safe in the back corner of the shelf.

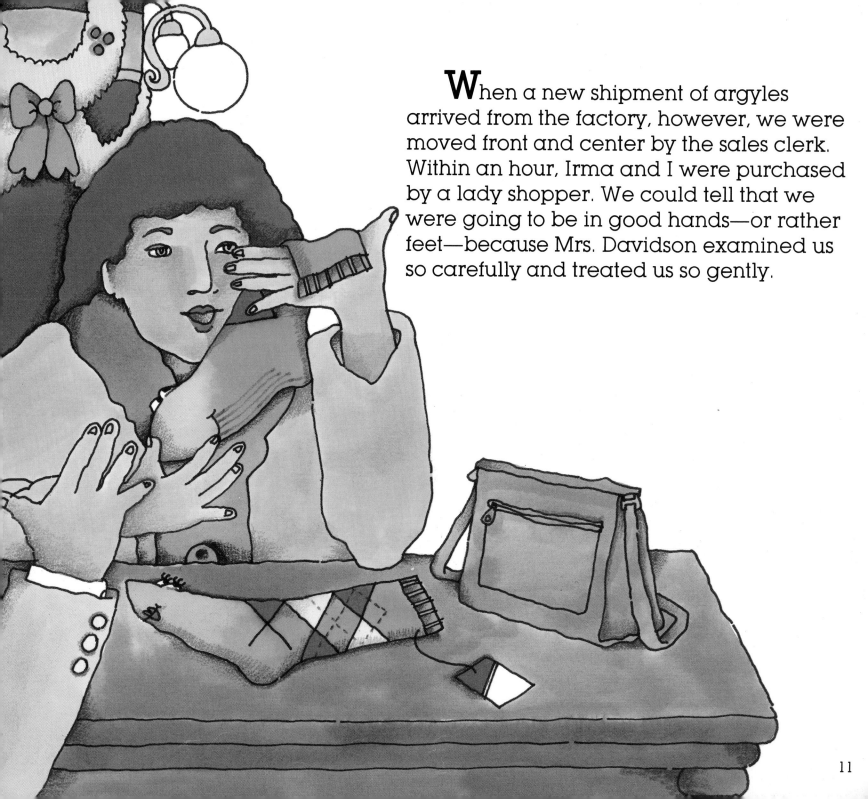

When a new shipment of argyles arrived from the factory, however, we were moved front and center by the sales clerk. Within an hour, Irma and I were purchased by a lady shopper. We could tell that we were going to be in good hands—or rather feet—because Mrs. Davidson examined us so carefully and treated us so gently.

It turned out that Mrs. Davidson had bought us for her son, Phil. Phil Davidson was a nice boy of ten. He wanted to be like his older brother, Bill, and that included wearing argyle socks. In the winter, Phil stayed inside a lot and practiced his violin. His feet were clean and his nails were neatly trimmed. But the hair on his legs tickled Irma and me. I loved to hear my Irma laugh.

Once when Phil had the chicken pox, he wore Irma and me for a week—on his hands. It was weird having a hand inside me for so long instead of a foot, but I knew that I was helping Phil, so I didn't mind. Irma didn't like it when Phil scratched himself. I told her to be patient.

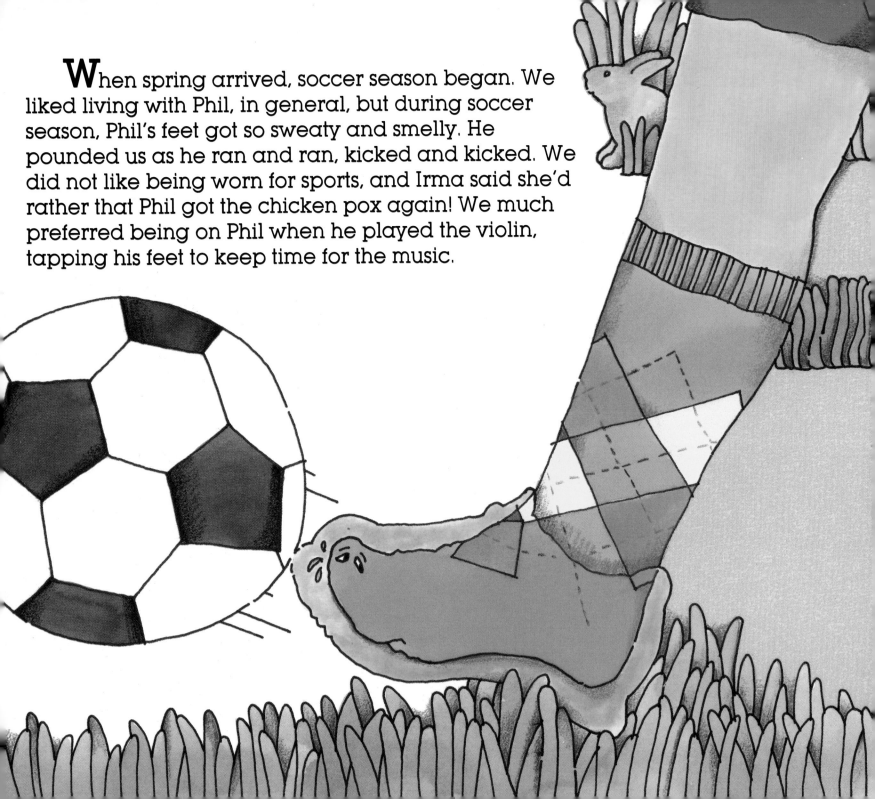

When spring arrived, soccer season began. We liked living with Phil, in general, but during soccer season, Phil's feet got so sweaty and smelly. He pounded us as he ran and ran, kicked and kicked. We did not like being worn for sports, and Irma said she'd rather that Phil got the chicken pox again! We much preferred being on Phil when he played the violin, tapping his feet to keep time for the music.

As we got older Phil wore us less and less, only for special occasions. I had to be darned twice, but Mrs. Davidson did a good job patching me. Actually, Mrs. Davidson had taken good care of us. She washed us by hand in soothing, warm water and bubbly soap.

When the weather was nice, Mrs. Davidson hung us out to dry on the clothesline in the backyard. The sunshine made us fluffy and fresh, and we were always in a good mood after a few hours of listening to the leaves rustling in the trees and the birds flying above.

The winters were hard on us because we were thrown into the dryer with the rest of the "delicate" laundry. For protection, we'd cling to the other garments as we swirled around and around inside the hot drum. The static electricity hurt when Mrs. Davidson had to pull us off her nightgown or off Mr. Davidson's handkerchiefs.

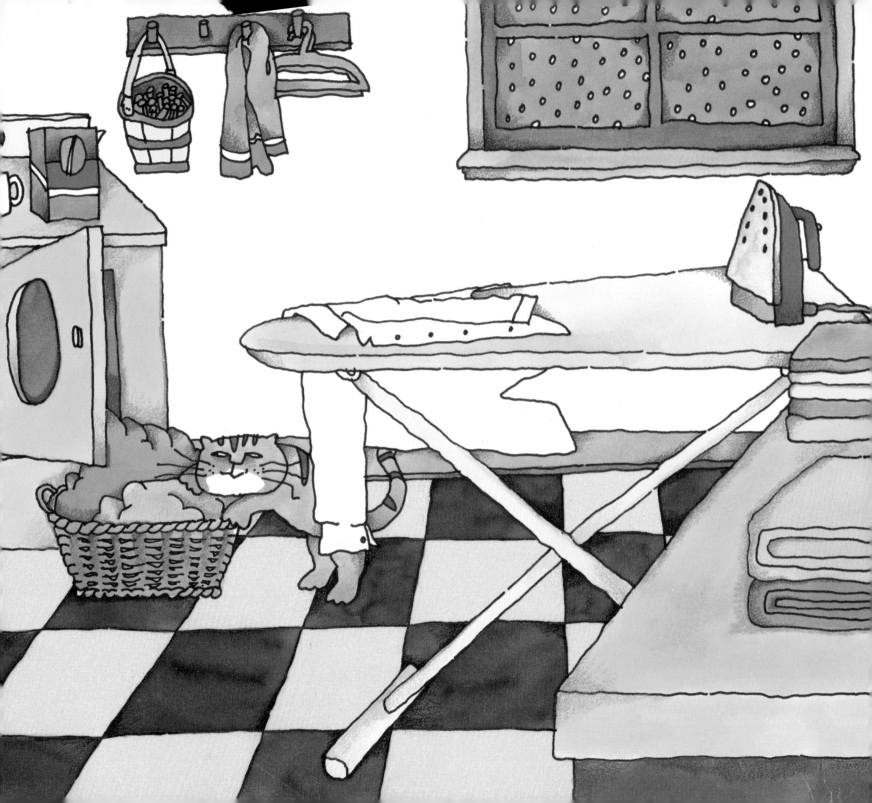

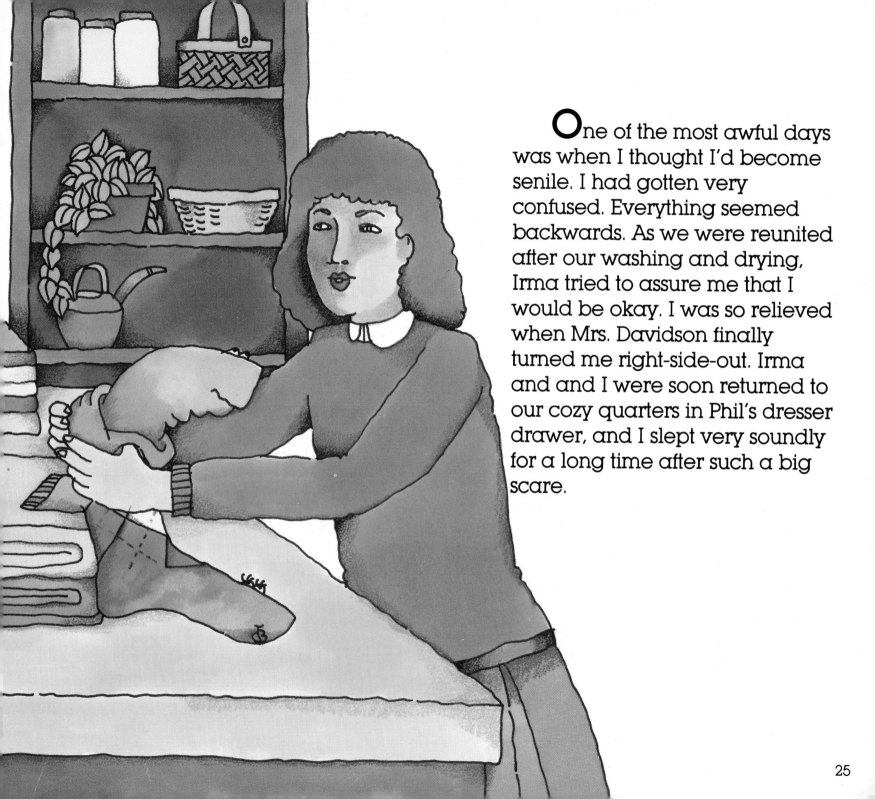

One of the most awful days was when I thought I'd become senile. I had gotten very confused. Everything seemed backwards. As we were reunited after our washing and drying, Irma tried to assure me that I would be okay. I was so relieved when Mrs. Davidson finally turned me right-side-out. Irma and and I were soon returned to our cozy quarters in Phil's dresser drawer, and I slept very soundly for a long time after such a big scare.

The last time I saw Irma was the day of Phil's music competition. He was very nervous, we could tell. Phil paced back and forth so much that I was getting dizzy. When he did sit down, he fidgeted so. Suddenly, he grabbed a thread on his other leg and absent-mindedly began to pull, and pull, and pull. Then a man came over and told Phil that his turn was next, so Phil broke off the thread, looked down to see what it came from, and realized that the pile of yarn on the floor was his unraveled left sock. Irma never had a chance.

Thank goodness Phil won the competition because he later told Mrs. Davidson that we were his lucky socks and she could not throw us out. Mrs. Davidson argued with Phil and they finally agreed that I could stay. Although I was sad and lonely, at least I didn't end up in the trash with Irma.

From that day on, Phil never wore me again. But whenever Phil has a soccer game or a music recital, he folds me up and puts me in his pocket just for luck. It's a lonely life now, without my dear Irma, but it's still exciting to be with Phil when his team wins a game or when he is on stage for a performance.

In a way, Irma's passing gave me a second chance, a new life. Sometimes an ending can be a beginning, too.

David Joel Klein is, in many respects, a very typical fourth grader. He always has too much homework but never enough time to play with his friends. When teacher Diane Koltnow directed her English class to write a story for the Akron, Ohio, Board of Education's Young Authors' Program, David waited until "the last minute" to begin the assignment. In fact, *Irwin the Sock* was born in tears of frustration and panic.

Mrs. Koltnow submitted all her students' stories to the Raintree **Publish-A-Book Contest**. On April 10, 1987, King Elementary School assembled to witness David receiving his award from Raintree Publishers. The ceremony was very special because it occurred not only on the last day of school before spring break (one whole week without homework!) but also two days before David's tenth birthday. In addition, David selected his brother, Adam Seth Klein, to read *Irwin the Sock* at the assembly.

Although the names "Irwin" and "Irma" have no special significance, many aspects of David's story relate to his family, friends, and personal experiences. For instance, David's grandfather, to whom this book is dedicated, was a broker of textile machinery and dealt with many factories in New England.

David's father, Steven Mark Klein, is Sports Editor of the *Lansing State Journal* and an adjunct journalism instructor at Michigan State University. David's mother, Linda Blauner Klein, is a self-employed tax consultant and financial planner.

The twenty second-prize winners of the Raintree **Publish-A-Book Contest** were: Janet Barkauskas, LaCrosse, Wisconsin; Christopher Battaglia, Buffalo, New York; Jeremy Chamberlin, Thompsonville, Michigan; Diana Clancy, Mystic, Connecticut; Vinh Dang, Huntington Beach, California; Ashley Emoto, Lawai, Hawaii; Lauren Feldman, Margate, New Jersey; Oceana Callum Feldman, Winters, California; Leanne Korszoloski, Wharton, New Jersey; John Rory Kropp, Manitowoc, Wisconsin; Avery Scott LaFleur, Rushford, Minnesota; Ella Lange, Havertown, Pennsylvania; Kristen Lynn Mann, Troy, New York; Russell Mantarro, Highland Park, New Jersey; Jenna Payne, Rohnert Park, California; Lynett Peugh, Zebulon, Georgia; Josh Pyle, Alma, Michigan; Rhonda Scoggins, Sharon, South Carolina; Vanessa Treps, Brown Deer, Wisconsin; and Ryan Zick, Milroy, Minnesota.

Artist Shirley Beckes was born in Columbus, Ohio, and now lives in the Milwaukee area with her husband David and daughter Jennifer. She has illustrated childrens books for the past fifteen years. She and her husband have their own design/illustration business in Mequon, Wisconsin.